SCHIRMER'S LIBRARY OF MUSICAL CLASSICS

Vol. 1296

HENRY ALTÈS

Twenty-Six Selected Studies

For the Flute

Edited by
GEORGE BARRÈRE

ISBN 978-0-7935-5422-5

G. SCHIRMER, Inc.

DISTRIBUTED BY

7777 W. BLUEMOUND RD. P.O. BOX 13819 MILWAUKEE, WI 53213

Copyright © 1918, 1945 (Renewed) by G. Schirmer, Inc. (ASCAP) New York, NY
International Copyright Secured. All Rights Reserved.
Warning: Unauthorized reproduction of this publication is
prohibited by Federal law and subject to criminal prosecution.

Twenty-Six
Selected Studies for Flute

From the Method by
HENRY ALTÈS

Edited by
George Barrère

Copyright © 1918, 1945 (Renewed) by G. Schirmer, Inc. (ASCAP) New York, NY
International Copyright Secured. All Rights Reserved.
Warning: Unauthorized reproduction of this publication is
prohibited by Federal law and subject to criminal prosecution.

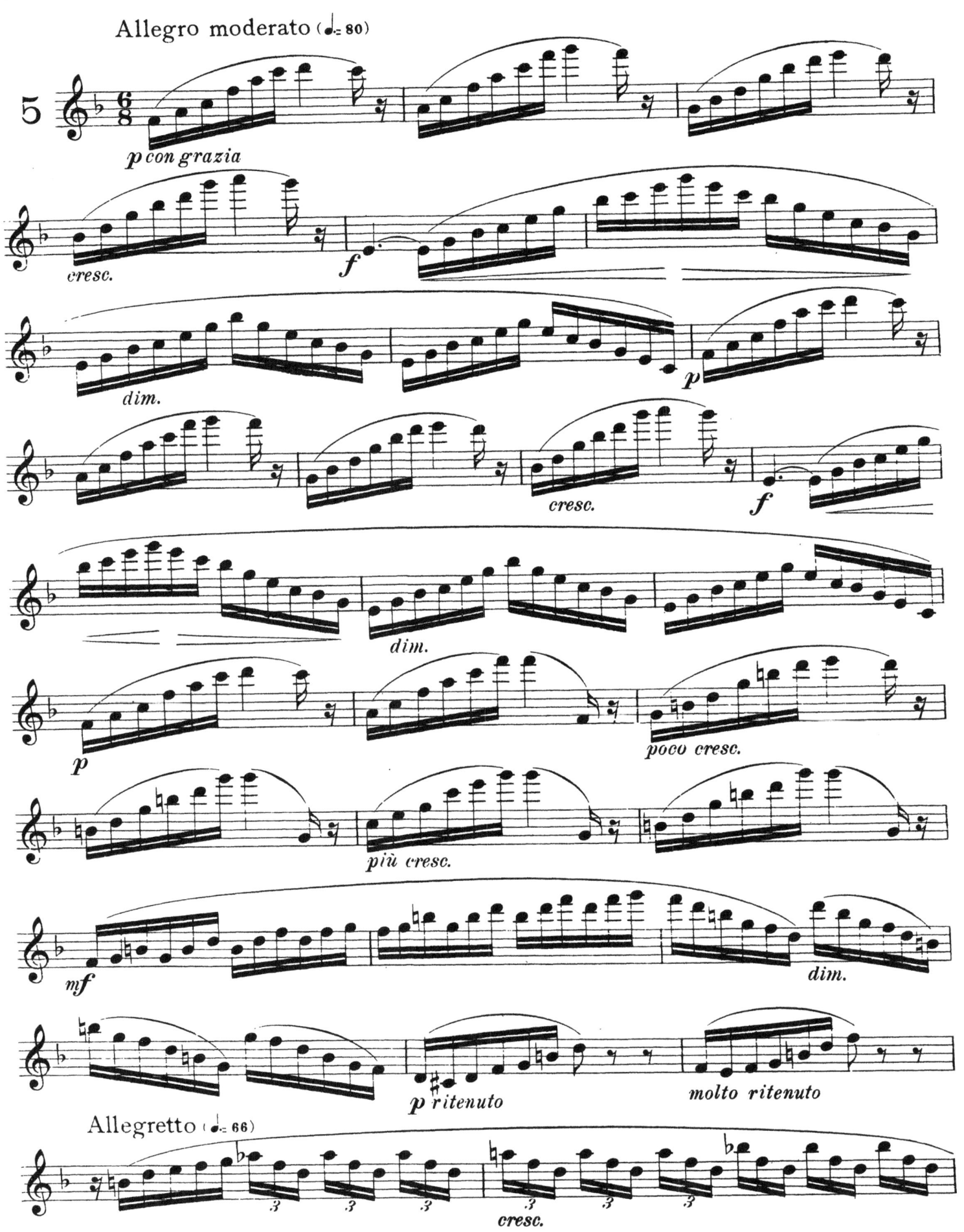

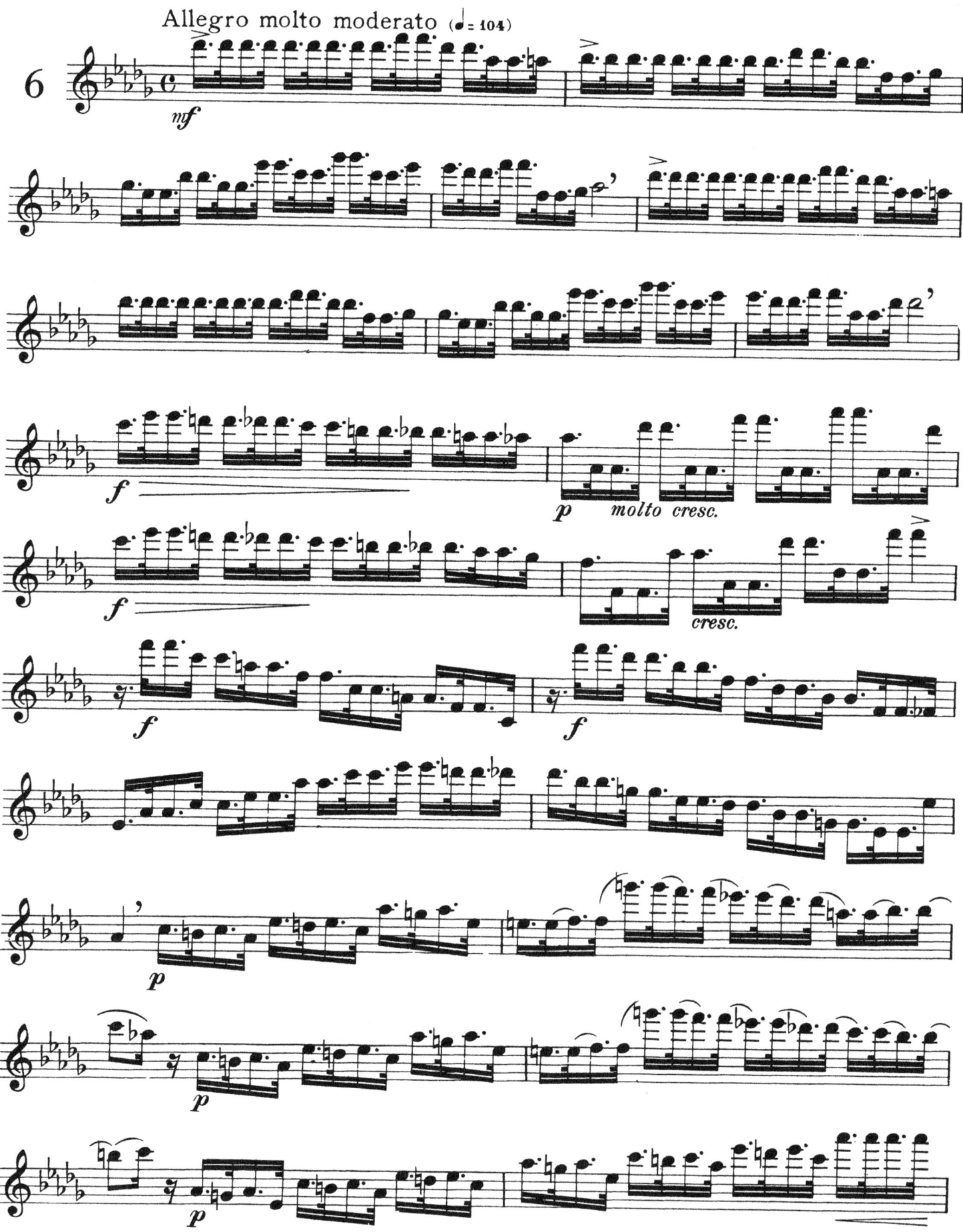

14

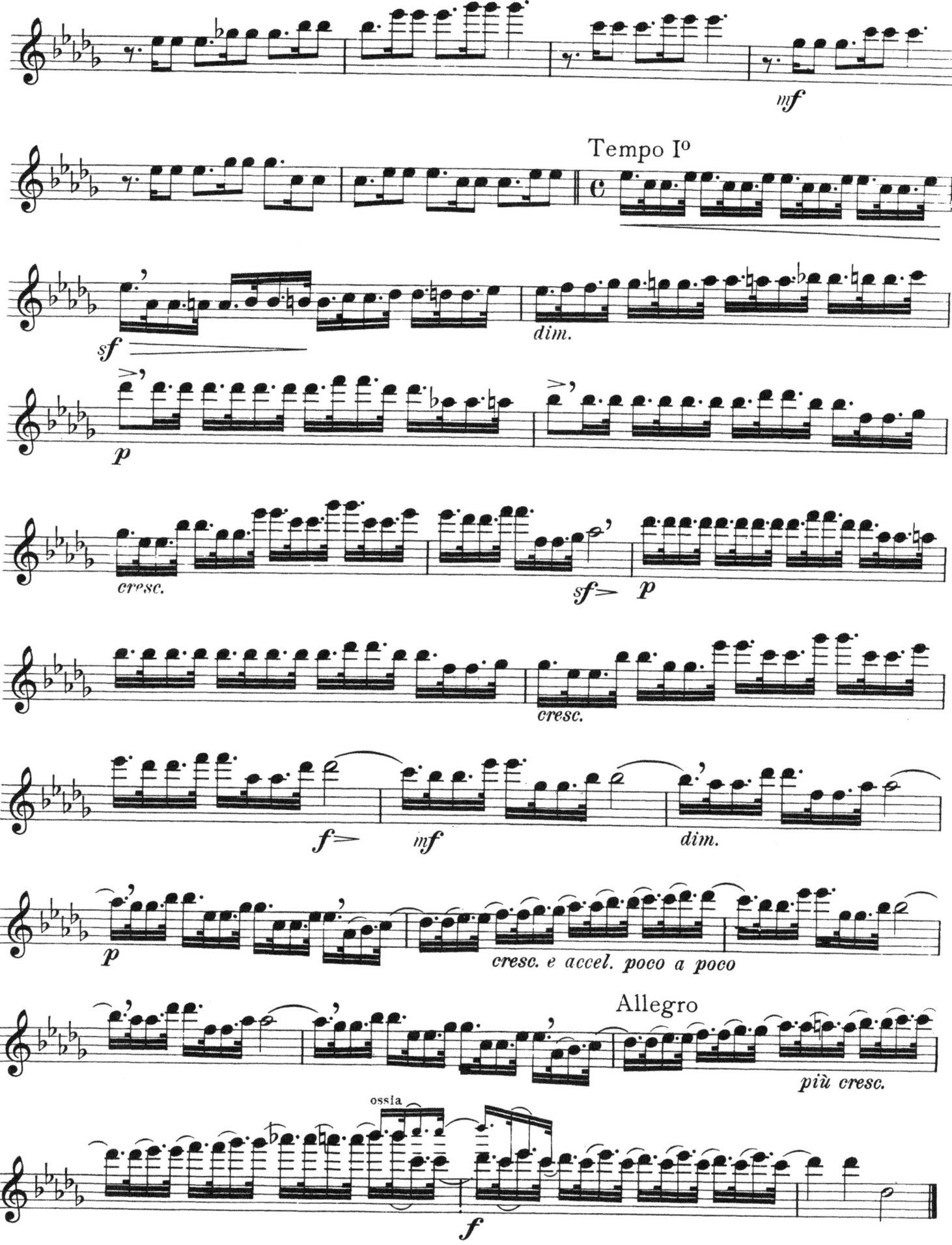

Introduction
Allegro (♩.= 66)

7

20

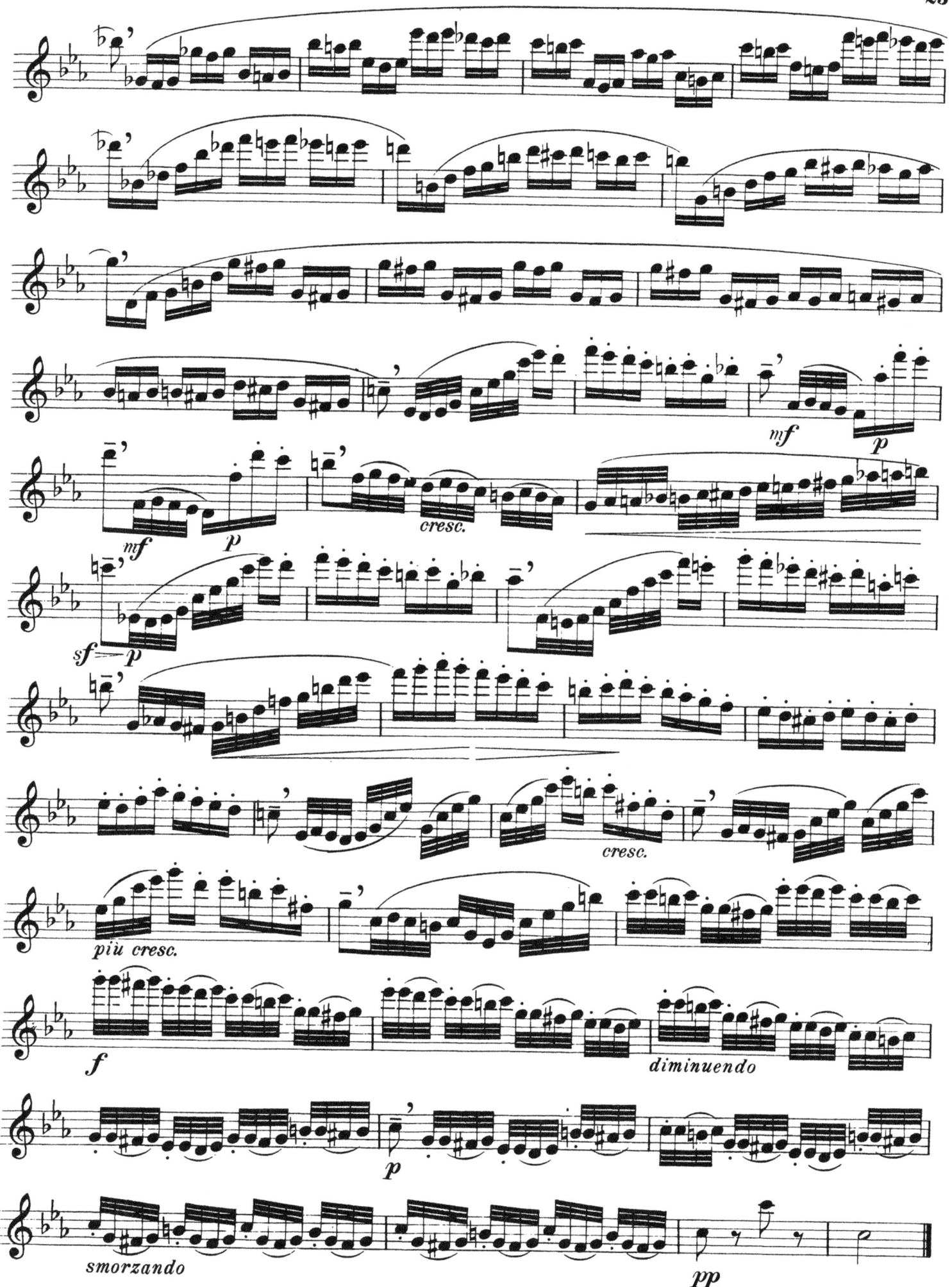

27

*) The passage from sign ✠ to sign ✠ is taken from the Ballet Music in Meyerbeer's opera, The Prophet

30

N.B. It will also be good practice to play this Study a semitone higher, in G Major.

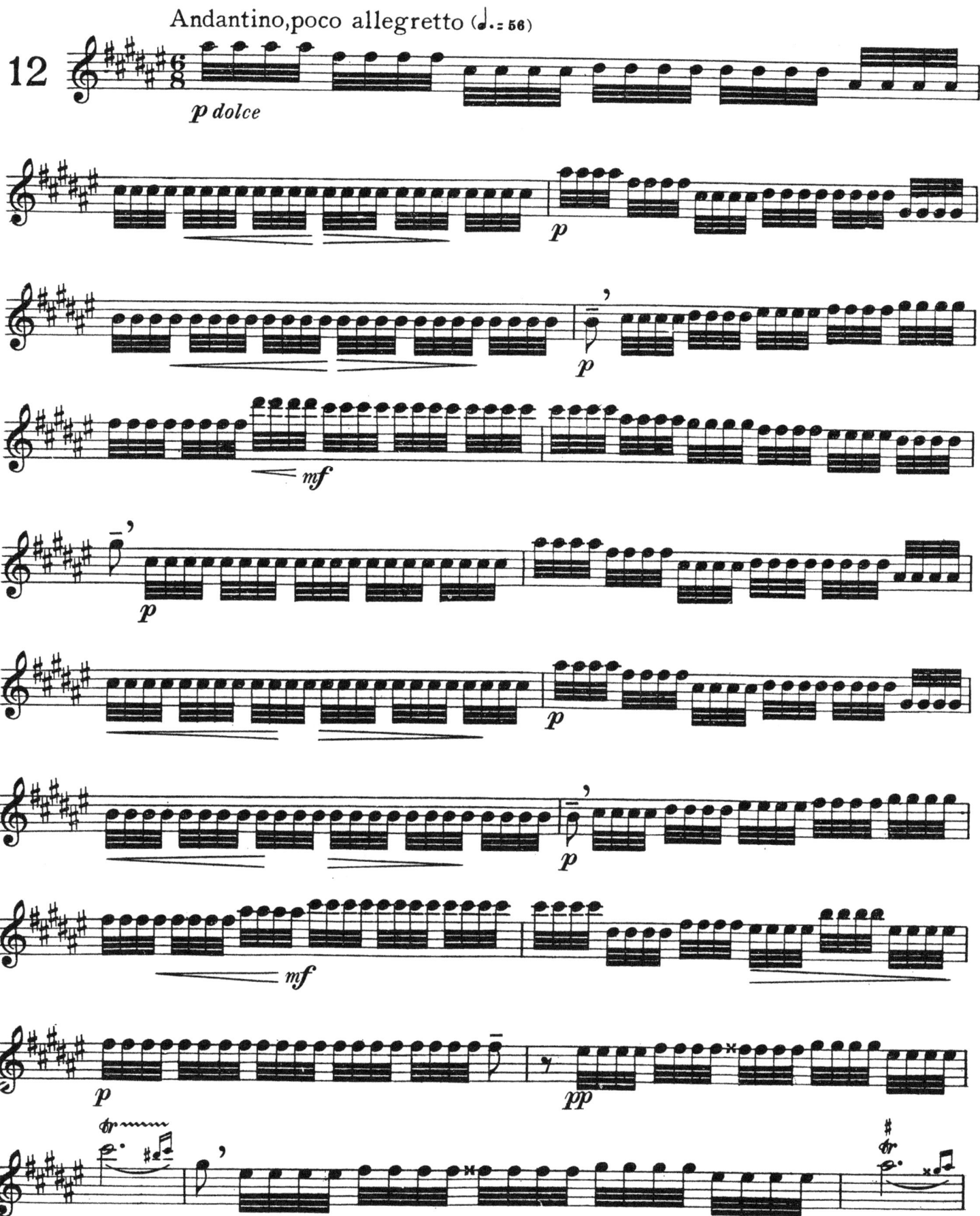

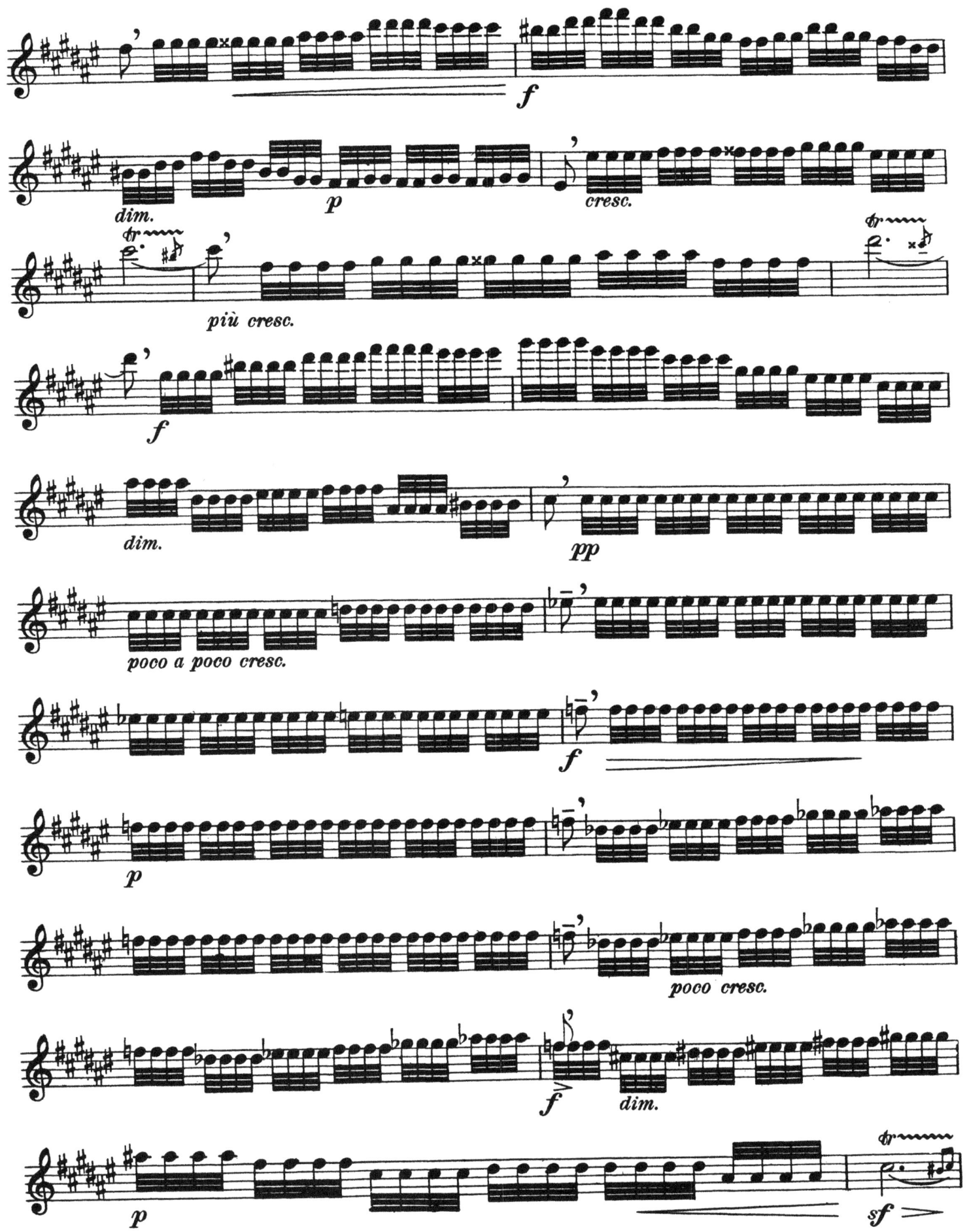

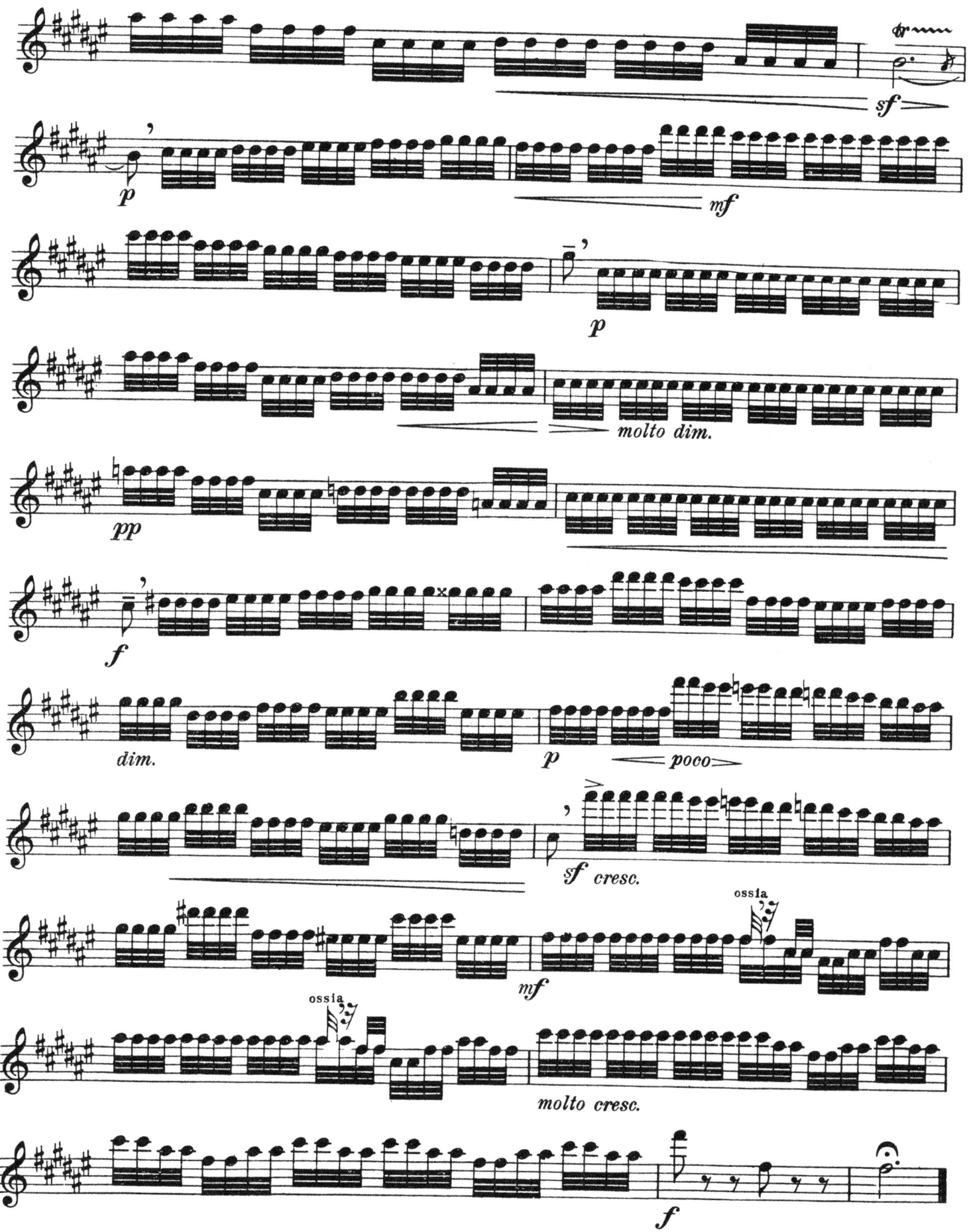

36

38

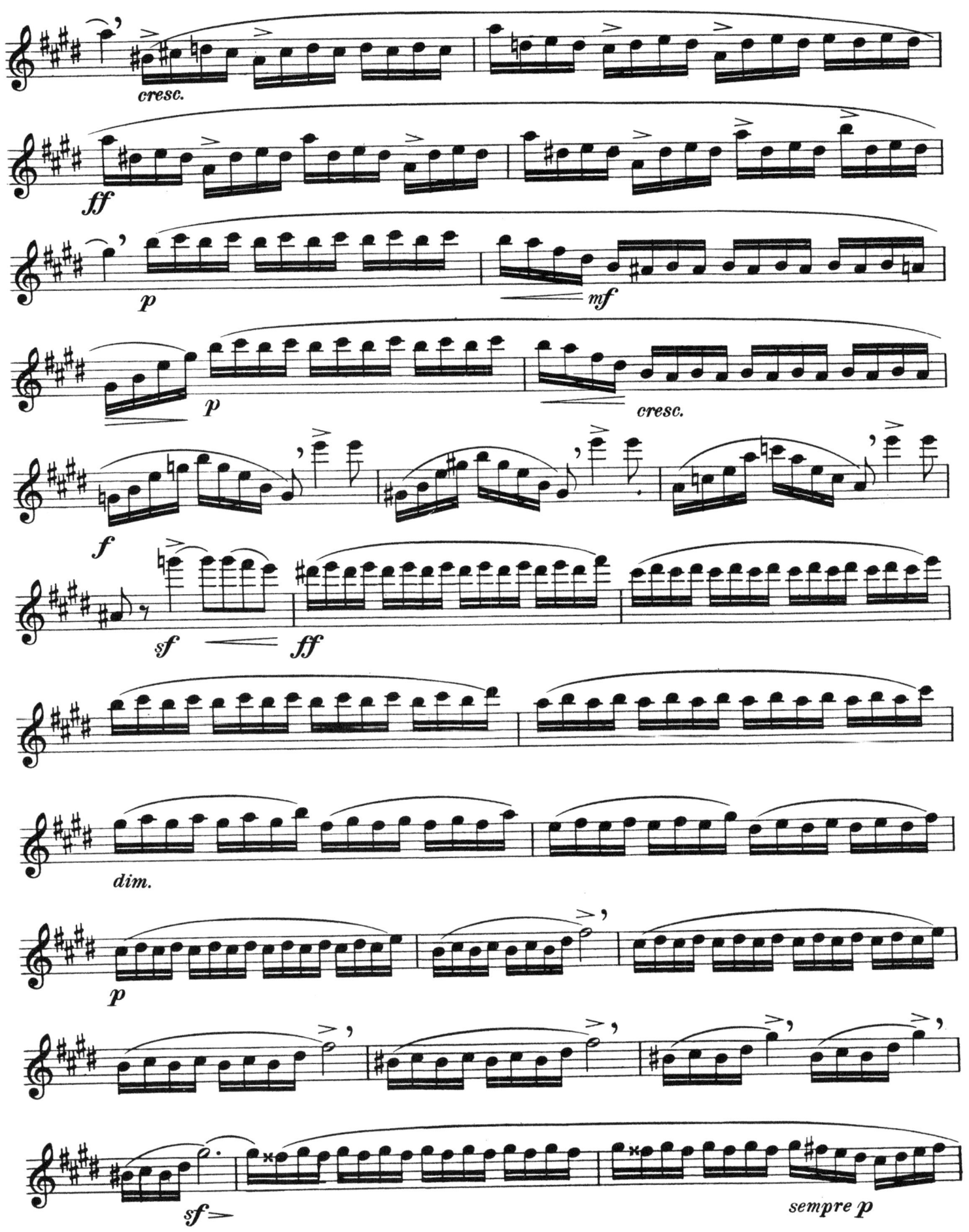

41

46

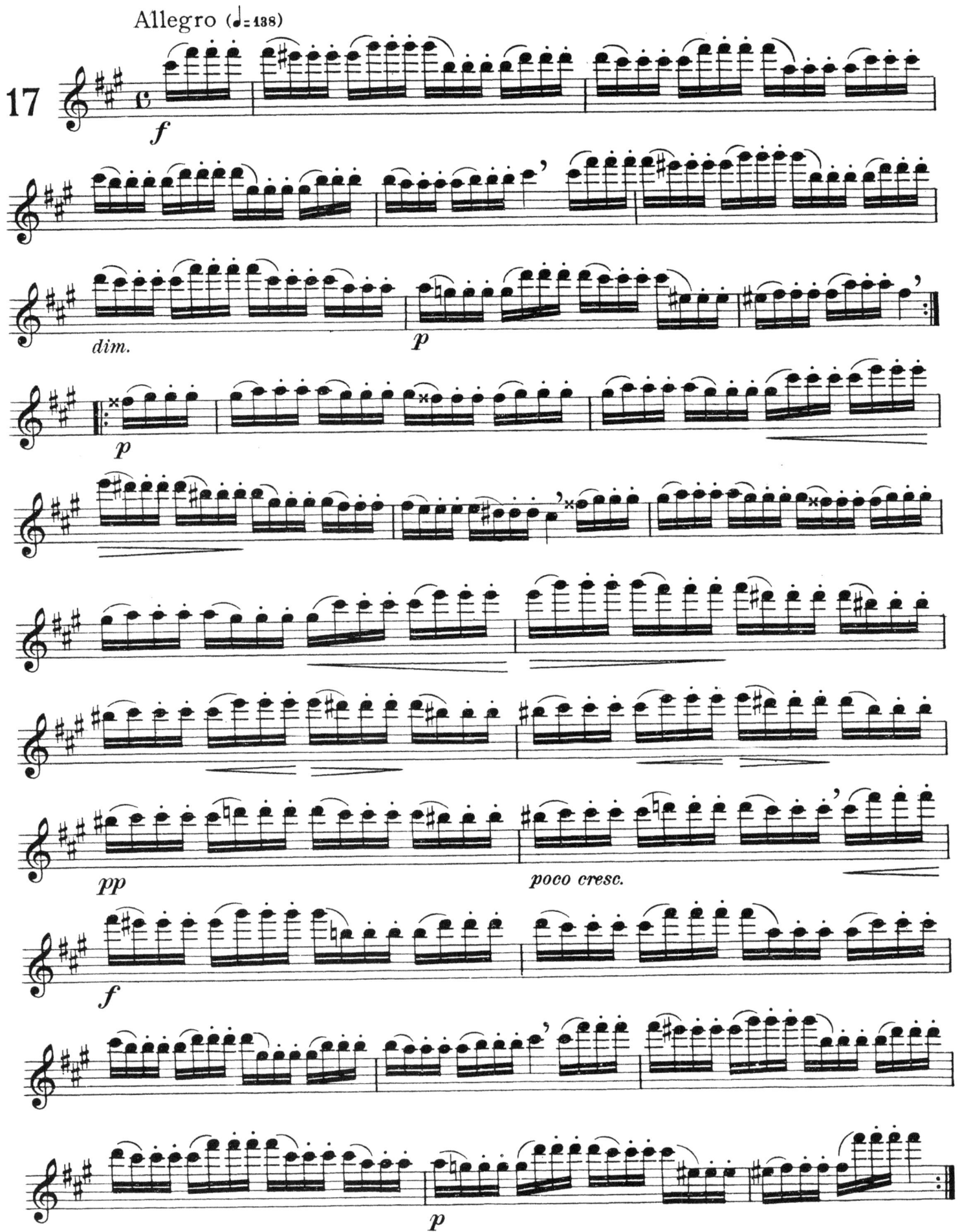

54

It will also be good practice to play this study transposed a semitone higher

N.B. This rather difficult study will be found easy to play if transposed half a tone higher

62

21 Allegro risoluto (♩=152)

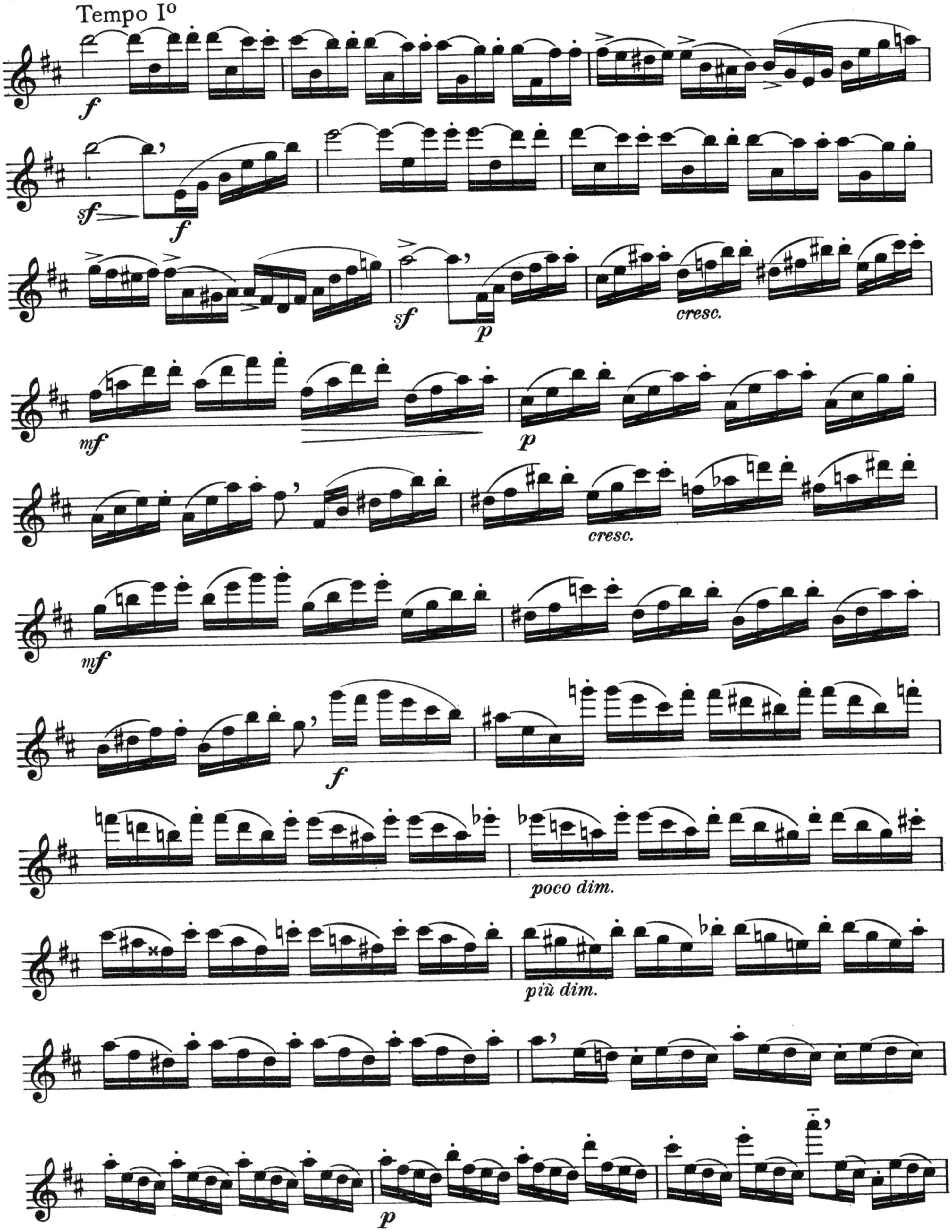
Tempo I°
f
sf
f
sf
p
cresc.
mf
p
cresc.
mf
f
poco dim.
più dim.
p

Scherzo from Mendelssohn's Midsummer Night's Dream
Transcription for two Flutes concertantes *

* The passages between these signs ⊢——⊣ are taken from the regular 1st and 2nd Flute-parts in the original orchestration.

75

78

N.B. This Study was written also one tone higher by the composer. Therefore it will be good practice to play it transposed into C major

82

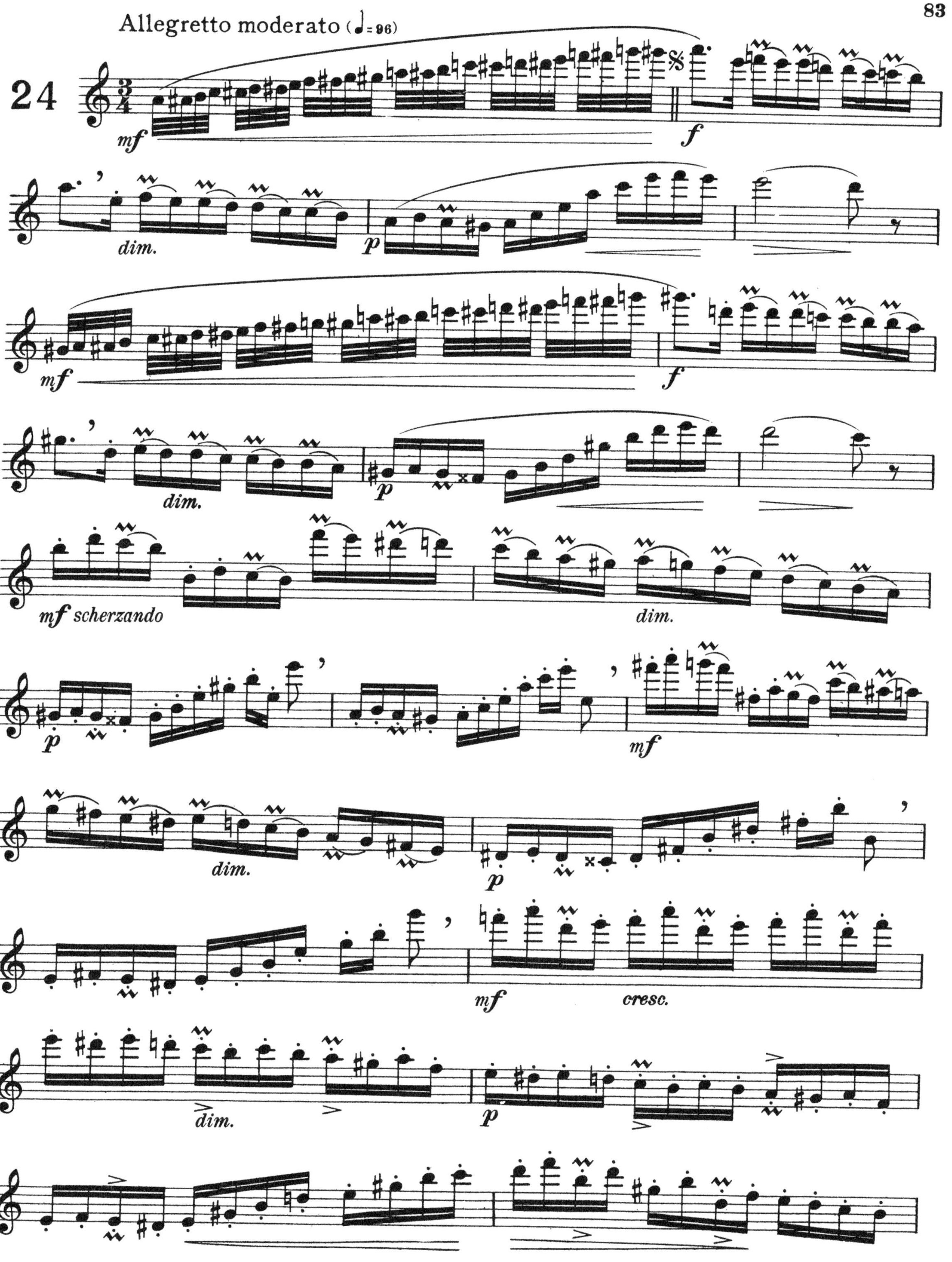
Allegretto moderato (♩= 96)
24
mf
f
dim.
p
mf
f
dim.
p
mf scherzando
dim.
p
mf
dim.
p
mf
cresc.
dim.
p

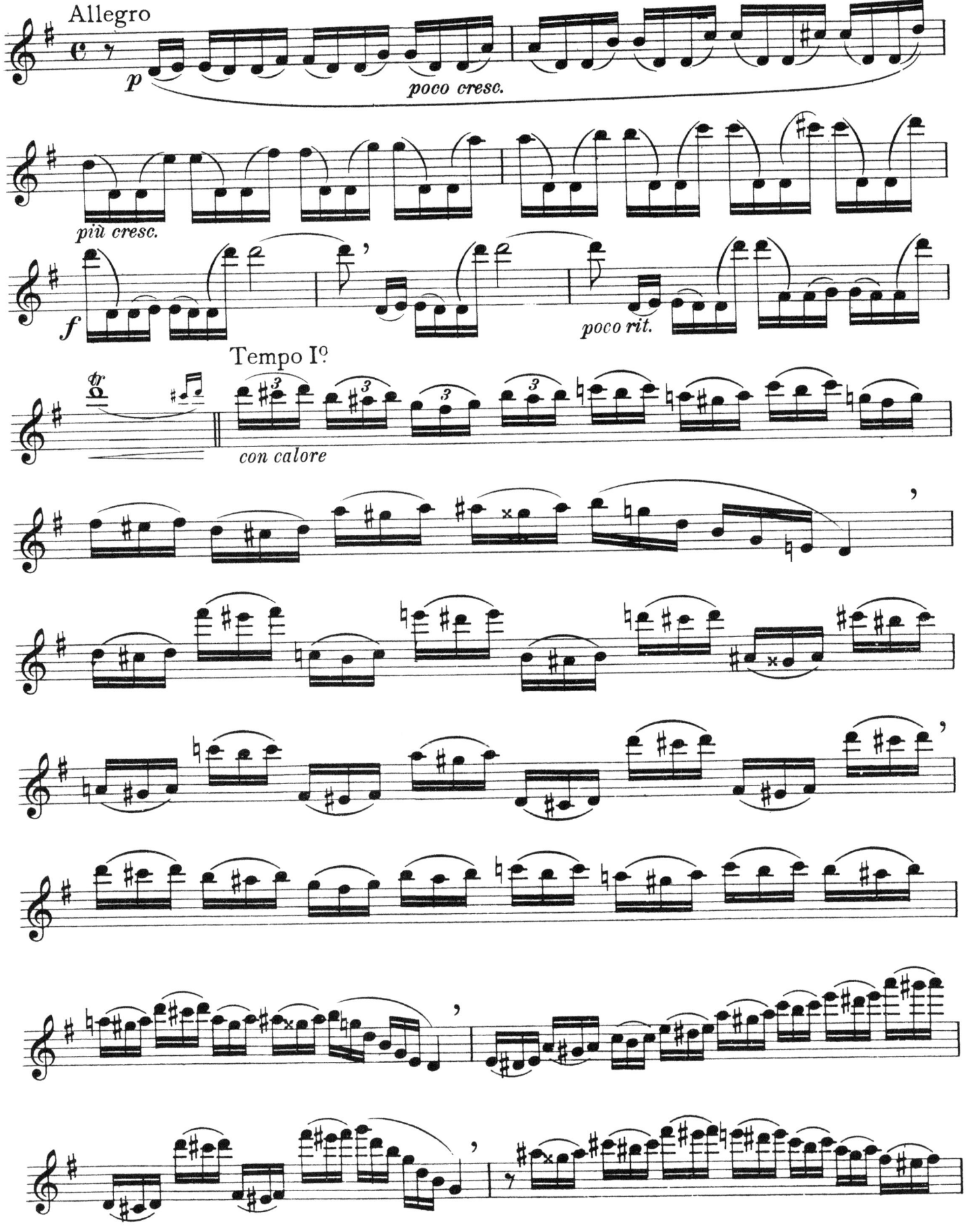

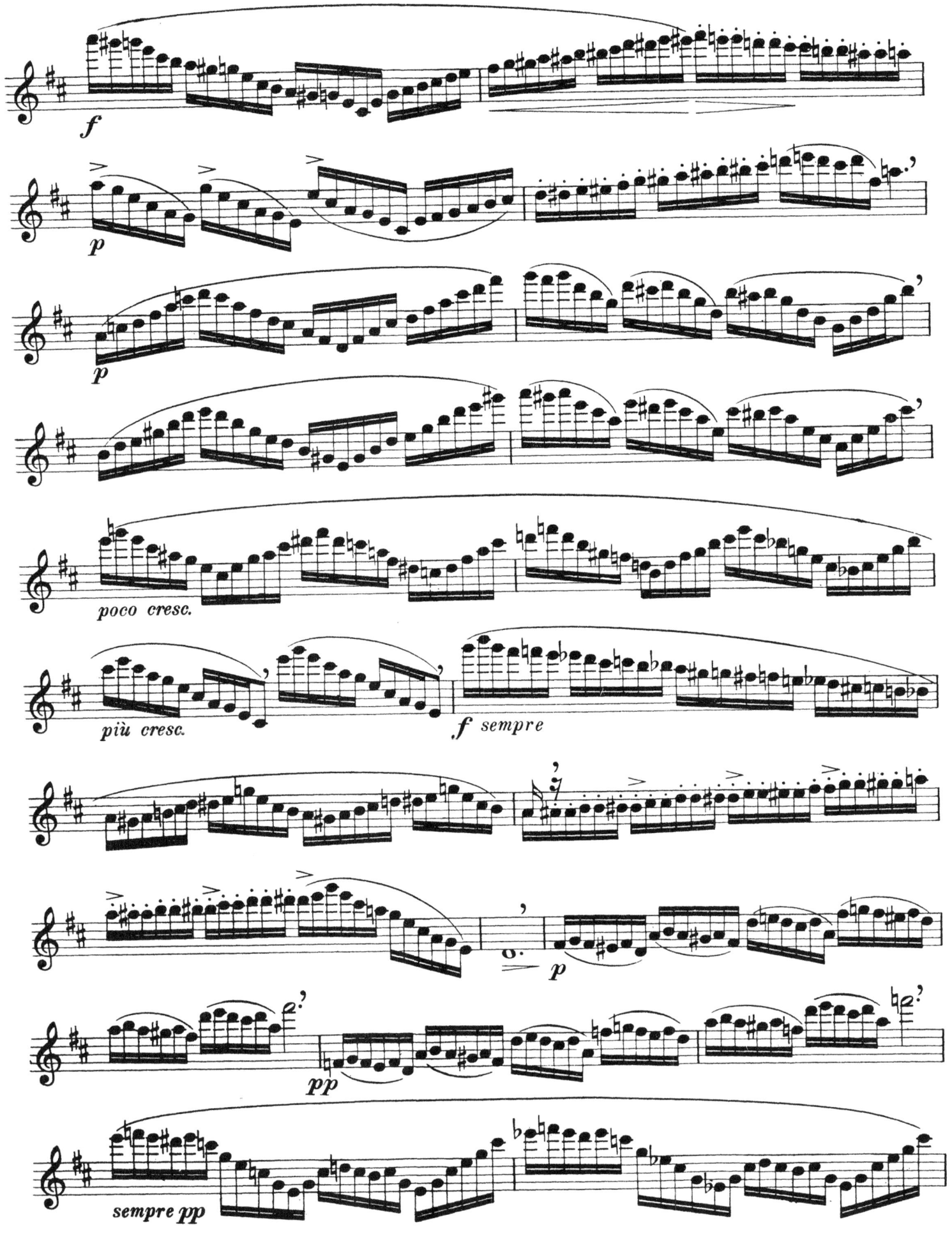

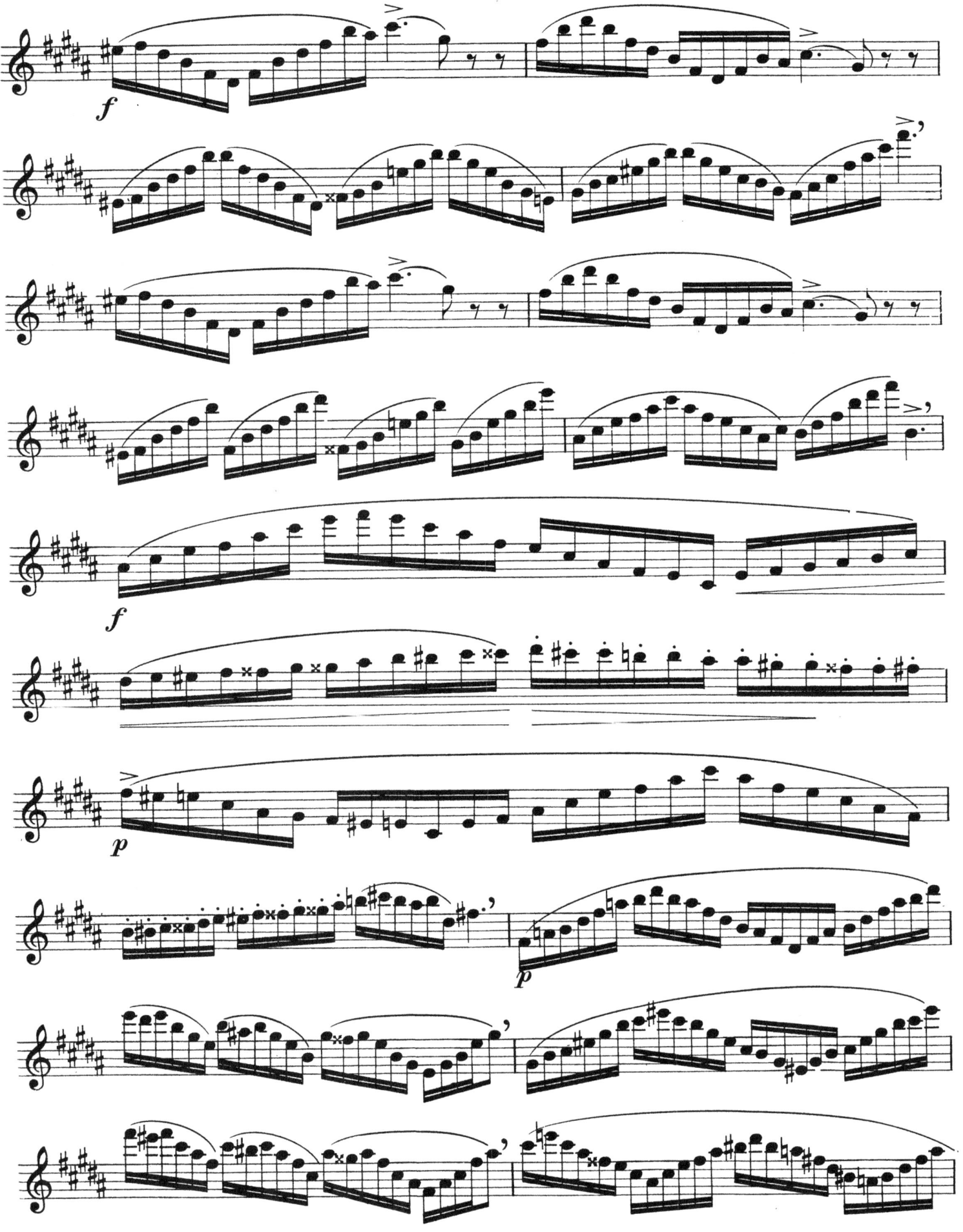

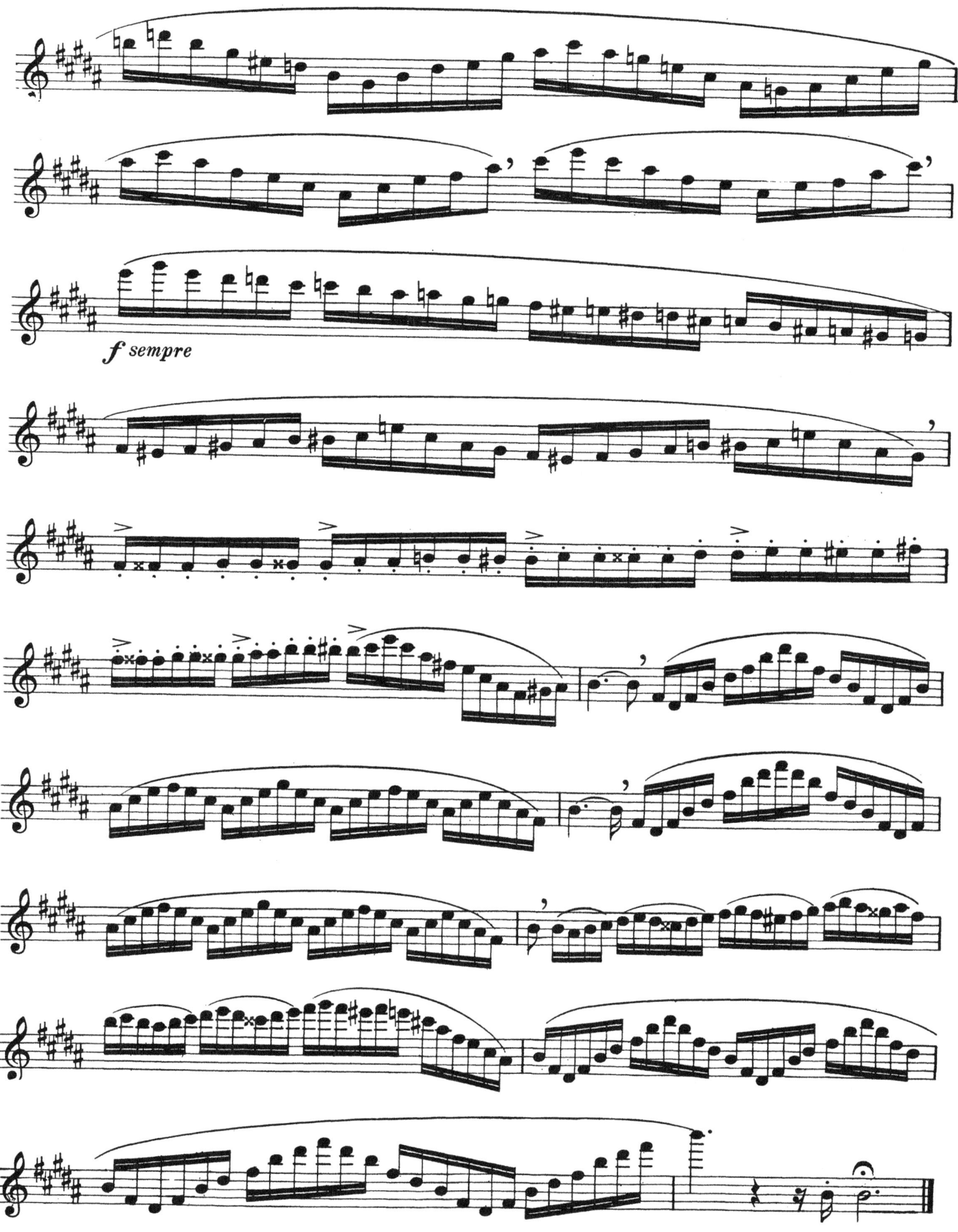